This book belongs to

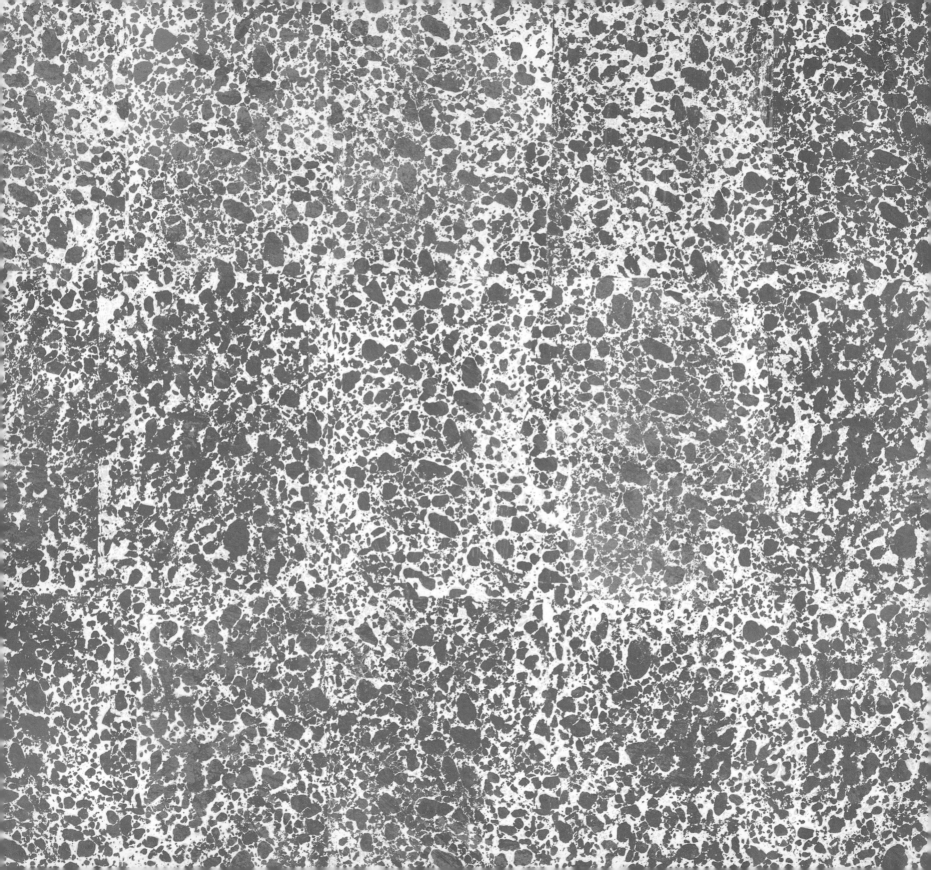

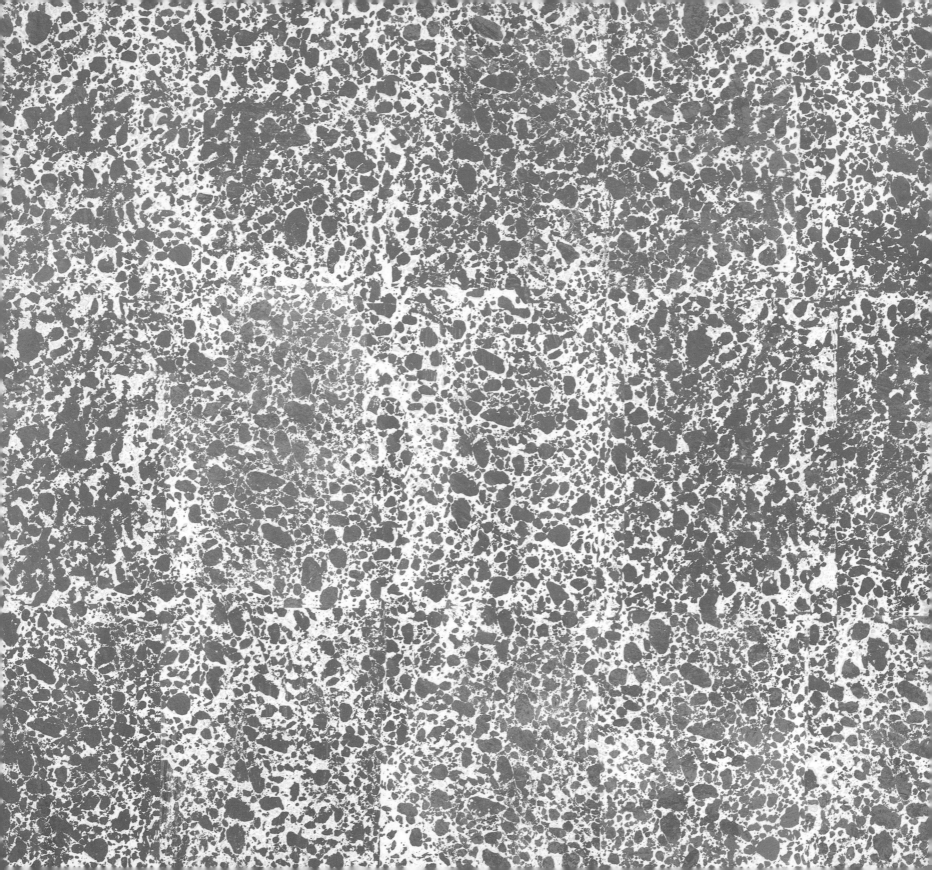

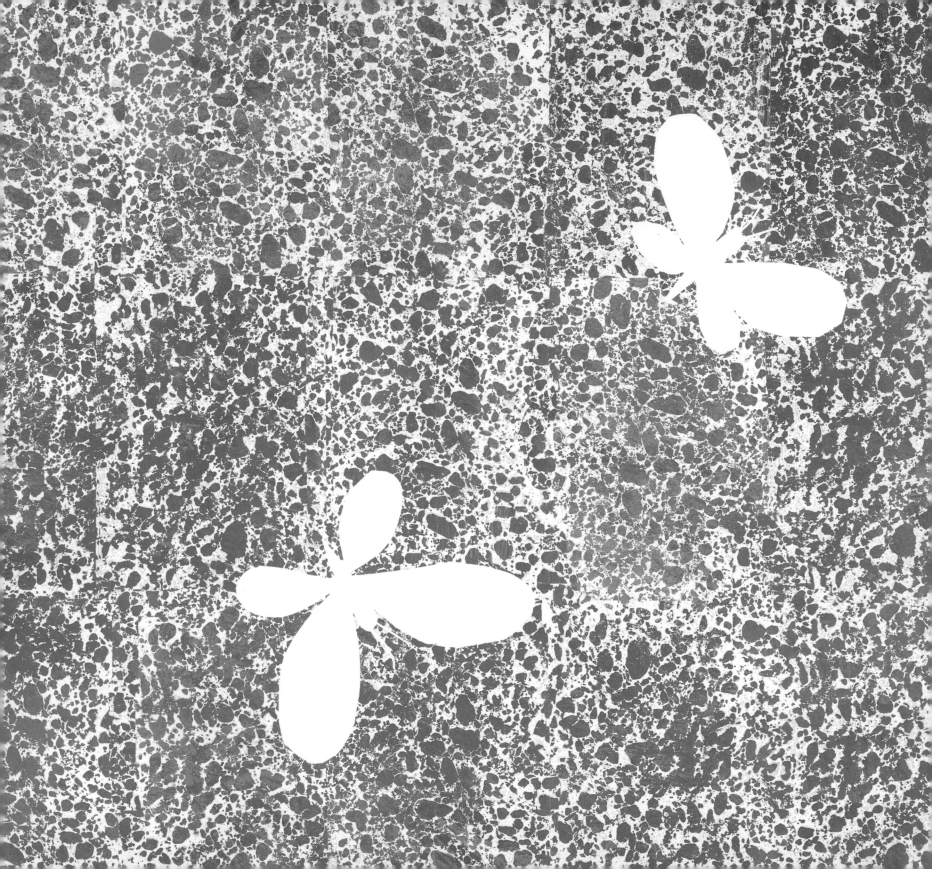

Kangaroo Christine

by Guido van Genechten

For all little ones who will let go of their moms
(and for all moms who manage to let go of their little ones)

tiger tales

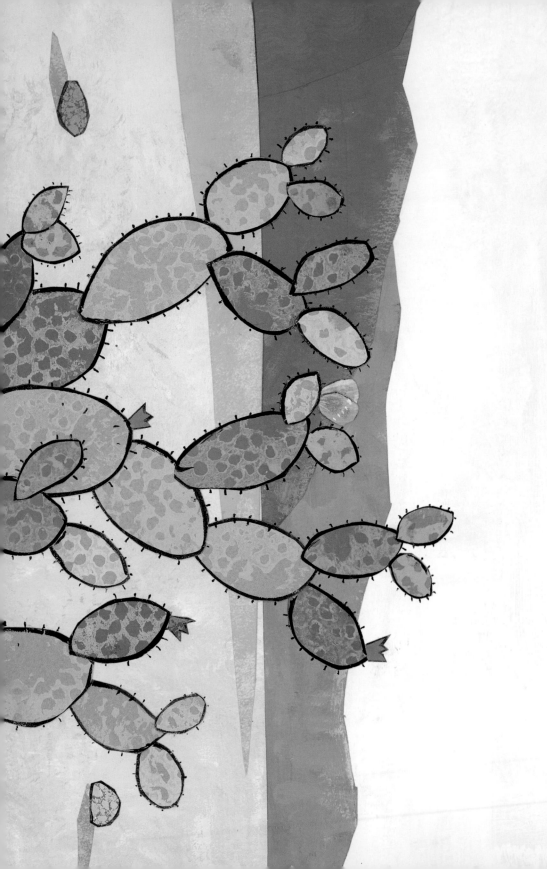

Mommy Kangaroo had a problem. Kangaroo Christine has grown too big for my pouch, she thought. It's time she hopped through life on her own legs.

But Kangaroo Christine didn't want to hop!
Her mommy's pouch was nice and soft,
and it kept them very close.

Mommy Kangaroo tried gently taking Kangaroo Christine out of her pouch.

But Kangaroo Christine went—HOP!—right back in.

"The world is a lot bigger than my pouch and much more exciting," Mommy Kangaroo said. "Look how the butterflies flutter from flower to flower."

"I don't care," said Kangaroo Christine. "I want to stay with you."

"Look how the elephants play in the water," Mommy Kangaroo said. "I don't like getting wet," said Kangaroo Christine. "I like your pouch where it's warm and dry."

"Listen to the birds whistling,"
Mommy Kangaroo tried. "I love to
dance when I hear them.
Don't you?"

"No, I don't," Kangaroo Christine said, even though she was tapping her foot. "I like listening to you hum instead."

"See how much fun the monkeys have swinging from tree to tree?" Mommy Kangaroo asked.

"I like monkeys, but swinging in trees looks dangerous," Kangaroo Christine said. "I'm safer in your pouch."

"Watch how fast the giraffes run across the plains," Mommy Kangaroo said.

"Giraffes are speedy," Kangaroo Christine agreed. "But the plains are too big for me. In your pouch, I know every little corner."

Exhausted, Mommy Kangaroo sat down. "More! More!" Kangaroo Christine cried out impatiently. "I want to see everything!" But Mommy Kangaroo could not take another step.

Just then, Kangaroo Christine saw someone in the distance jumping closer and closer.
Those are the best and longest hops I've ever seen, she thought.

The hopper came right up to Kangaroo Christine.
He had the same nose, the same ears, the same legs,
and even the same strong tail as she!
"I'm Ben," he said. "Do you want to play?"

"Yes!" said Kangaroo Christine. "Will you
teach me how to jump just like you do?"
Then she hopped out
of Mommy Kangaroo's
pouch. . . .

and into the wide world.

Finally, Mommy Kangaroo's pouch was empty. "Don't go too far!" Mommy Kangaroo called, as Kangaroo Christine kept on hopping and hopping and hopping. . . .

tiger tales
an imprint of ME Media, LLC
202 Old Ridgefield Road, Wilton, CT 06897
Published in the United States 2006
Originally published as *Hoe Kleine Kangoeroe de wereld in sprong in Belgium* 2005
By Uitgeverij Clavis, Hasselt—Amsterdam
Copyright ©2005 Uitgeverij Clavis, Hasselt—Amsterdam
CIP data is available
ISBN 1-58925-396-5
Printed in China
All rights reserved
1 3 5 7 9 10 8 6 4 2